MY CREATURE TEACHER

My Creature Teacher

www.harperchildrens.com

Library of Congress Cataloging-in-Publication Data
Leuck, Laura.
My creature teacher / by Laura Leuck ; illustrated by Scott Nash.—1. ed.
p. cm.
Summary: A student describes all the things that
his creature teacher does at school.
ISBN 0-06-029694-1 — ISBN 0-06-029695-X (lib. bdg.)
[1. Teachers—Fiction. 2. Monsters—Fiction
3. Schools—Fiction. 4. Stories in rhyme.]
I. Nash, Scott, ill. II. Title.
PZ8.3.L565 Myd 2003
[E]—dc21 2002005644
Typography by Stephanie Bart-Horvath
1 2 3 4 5 6 7 8 9 10
❖
First Edition

To my beautiful sister, Amy
—L.L.

For Beasty Baby Ben,
from your Ugly Uncle Scott

10

MY CREATURE TEACHER

by Laura Leuck
illustrated by Scott Nash

HarperCollins*Publishers*

My creature teacher's strict and stern—
she growls so I will wait my turn.
If we want to howl or shriek
we MUST put up our paws to speak.

She likes to keep our classroom grim
by draping poison ivy trim,

TODAY'S LESSON:
things that crawl

and pinning thorns upon the wall,
and filling desks with things that crawl.

She makes us hang our spider sacks

and put away our creepy snacks.

She won't accept the taped and glued

assignments that my werewolf chewed.

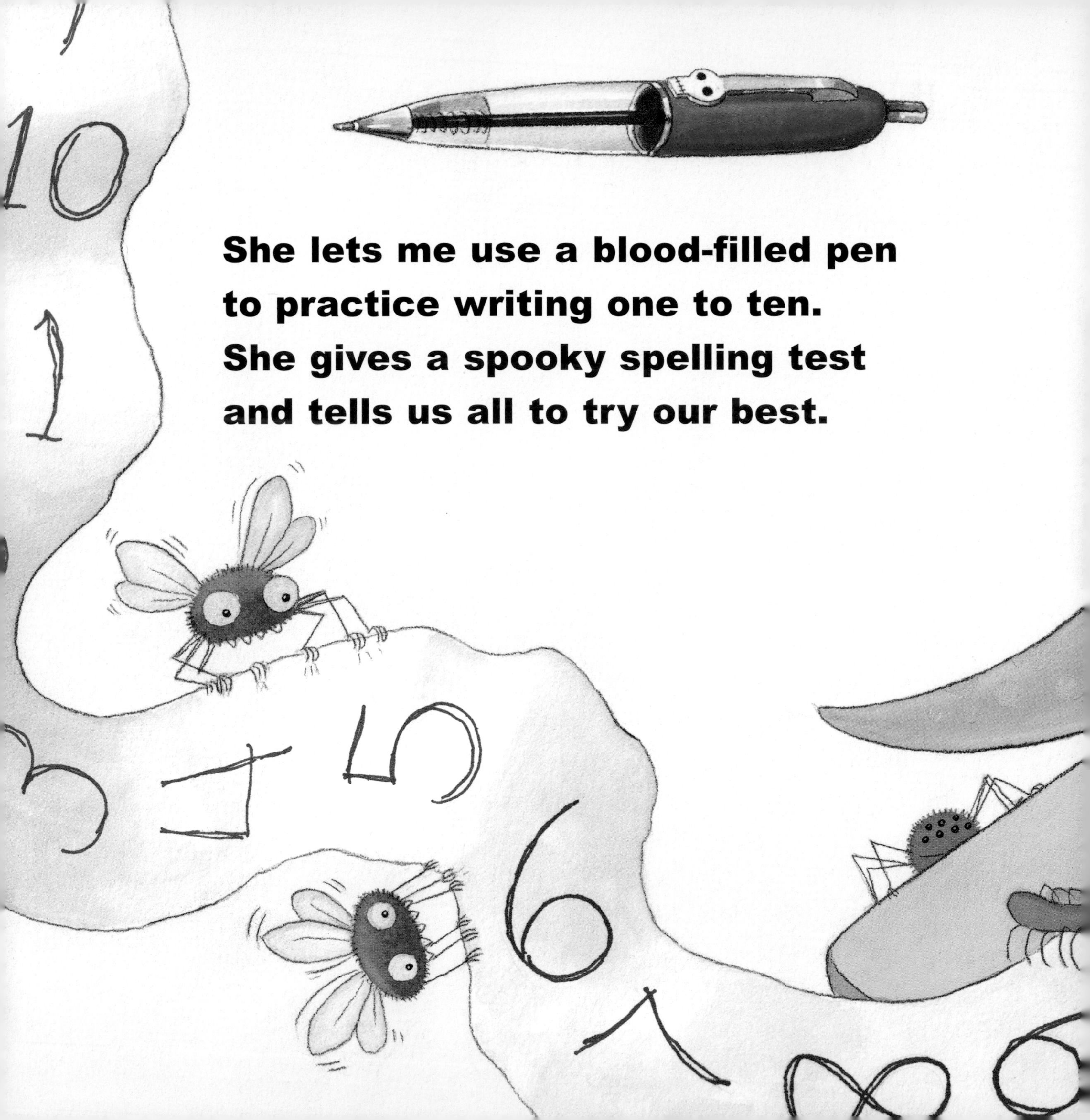

She lets me use a blood-filled pen
to practice writing one to ten.
She gives a spooky spelling test
and tells us all to try our best.

**At crunch time, when we sit and eat
she wants me staying in my seat,
and sometimes lets me swap or trade
the handwich that my mother made.**

She turns her head around to see
the beastly bully pick on me.
She sees him snatch my beetle ale
and dump it in the garbage pail.

She sends the
bully on a broom
straight to the mean
headmonster's room,

then chooses ME to go and get

our fire-breathing classroom pet.

She takes us out for recess time to jump and play in piles of slime.

We climb some rotten apple trees

and dangle by our
fuzzy knees.

And when the late-day vulture sings,
she helps us grab our gruesome things,
then puts us on the ghoul school bus.
I'm glad my teacher's there for us!

GHOUL SCHOOL

So if your creature teacher's near—
thank her for her help this year!